W9-AJP-923

For Aunt Gussie, our very own Dancing Granny
—E.W.

For Larry and Jeff
—S.M.

Dancing Granny

by Elizabeth Winthrop

GRANNY'S GIFT SHOPPE

VILLE

illustrated by Salvatore Murdocca

I asked my granny to the zoo.
"I'd rather not," she said.
"My nightie's on, my teeth are out.
I think I'll stay in bed."

"Now come with me, my granny, please.
Don't fuss and fret like that."
I stuffed her in her party shoes
and found her big straw hat.

"I told the animals to wait,
I told them you'd be there!
The elephant has had a bath,
the lion has combed his hair.

We're going to have a party now,
we plan to have a dance.
The monkeys asked their relatives.
They just flew in from France."

"I think you're full of silliness,
you must have gone quite mad.
I'm much too old for parties, though
my dancing isn't bad.

These horrid shoes are pinching tight,
I must undo my bun.
You leave me here where I belong,
go on and have your fun."

"You are a goose, my granny, dear."
I kissed her on her nose.
I took her pinching shoes away
and kissed her on her toes.

I put her purple sneakers on,
the ones she loves to wear.
I washed her face and trimmed her nails
and brushed her long gray hair.

I took my granny to the zoo,
her hand all curled in mine.
The whistle blew, the bright flags flew,
her eyes began to shine.

"At last!" they cried when we arrived.
The monkeys climbed the gate,
the snakes and tigers tangled up,
the ostrich growled, "You're late."

ZOO

7

The bear waltzed up to Granny, then
he whispered in her ear,
"Pleased to meet you, glad to know you,
happy that you're here."

He took ahold of Granny's hand
and led us through the crowd.
The parrot squawked, the hippo hopped,
the rhino stamped and bowed.

The cage doors all flew open when
the band began to play.
The lion blew his big brass horn,
Granny began to sway.

The bear asked, "May I have this dance?"
He led her to the floor.
He picked her up and twirled her 'round,
then twirled her 'round once more.

My granny was delighted.
Her face turned bright beet red.
She leapt and jumped, she kicked her heels,
she twice stood on her head.

Six silly monkeys waltzed with her,
the snake curled 'round her shoes.
She danced with each and every one
to jazz and swing and blues.

At last the party was over.
We fell down in a heap.
The lion put his horn away,
the ostrich went to sleep.

The bear took Granny by her arm,
he led her to the train.
The others lined up side by side
to wave good-bye again.

"You'll come again, you won't forget?"
the eager bear called out.
She shut her eyes, she pursed her lips
and kissed him on his snout.

The train rocked back and forth that night.
I took a little nap.
My shoes were off, my eyes were closed,
my head in Granny's lap.

"I'm free next week," my granny said.
She stroked my tangled hair.
"It would be grand to come again
and rhumba with the bear."

Her sneakered feet tapped such a beat.
She sang a silly tune
of dancing pairs and handsome bears
under the silver moon.

Marshall Cavendish, 99 White Plains Road, Tarrytown, NY 10591
www.marshallcavendish.com

Library of Congress Cataloging-in-Publication Data
Winthrop, Elizabeth.
Dancing Granny / written by Elizabeth Winthrop;
illustrated by Salvatore Murdocca.
p. cm.
Summary: Granny and her grandchild take a nighttime trip
to the zoo, where the animals have prepared a fabulous
party and Granny dances the night away.
ISBN 0-7614-5141-2
[1. Grandmothers—Fiction. 2. Dance—Fiction. 3. Zoos—Fiction.
4. Zoo animals—Fiction. 5. Stories in rhyme.] I. Murdocca, Sal, ill. II. Title.
PZ8.3.W727Dan 2003   [E]—dc21   2002154717

This book is set in 17-point Sassoon Primary.
The illustrations are rendered in ink, watercolor, and color pencil.
Book design by Adam Mietlowski

Printed in China
First edition
2 4 6 5 3 1